To Govins
Nov, 3, 1989
Happy 4th Birthday
Love,
Emma

For Beatrice

SIMON AND SCHUSTER
BOOKS FOR YOUNG READERS
Simon & Schuster Building, Rockefeller Center
1230 Avenue of the Americas, New York, New York 10020

10 9 8 7 6 5 4 3 2 1

ISBN 0-671-67683-0

~ BUDGIE ~
The Little Helicopter

H.R.H. The Duchess of York
Illustrated by John Richardson

SIMON AND SCHUSTER BOOKS FOR YOUNG READERS

PUBLISHED BY SIMON & SCHUSTER INC., NEW YORK

It was a hot, hot day. Budgie, the helicopter, was bored. He looked around the huge hangar but nothing stirred. Oliver, the owl, was fast asleep and even Fergus, the cat, didn't notice the mouse in front of his nose. Budgie turned on his radio but nothing was happening.

Every now and then he cooled himself with a whirr of his rotors. "Same old faces," he thought, as he looked around. "I wish something exciting would happen." Budgie always longed for a bit of adventure.

Yesterday Budgie spent the whole day delivering crate
after crate of clawing lobsters from Mulhearn-on-Sea.
"I may be the littlest helicopter," he sighed to himself, "but
I wish I wasn't always given the nastiest little jobs to do."

How Lionel, the Lynx, laughed when Budgie was forced to have a thorough wash and polish afterwards, because he smelled so fishy. There was nothing Budgie disliked more than a good scrub in the helicopter wash.

Clatter, clatter, clatter, blatter, blatter, clatter.
Budgie looked up and saw Lionel.
"Hurumph!" Lionel cleared his throat. "Hurumph! Um, this is
Budgie," he said to a small plane who sparkled and shone.

"He's not usually so clean. Must have been forced to wash."
Budgie blushed red to the roots of his rotors.
"I'm Pippa," said the plane. "I'm new."
"Hello," smiled Budgie.

Bang! Bang! Bang! went the bird scarer. Everyone jumped.
"That's for me. Today is my first flight," said Pippa.
"May I come?" said Budgie. "It looks as though there might be a

thunderstorm and I can warn you if there's any danger of lightning."

"Oh, thank you," said Pippa. "Let's go."

"It's all right for you," groaned Lionel. "Some of us have real work to do."

Pippa soared. She looped the loop. *Wheeee.* Flew on her side. *Brrrr.*

Then swooped. *Eoww.* "Hurrah, hurrah," shouted Budgie. "Well done, Pippa!"

Just then there was a loud noise. *Whoop, whoop, whoop,*
it went. *Whoop, whoop, whoop.*
"That's the alarm," said Budgie.
"Control calling Lionel. Control calling Lionel.

Lionel come in please. Emergency, Lionel. Over."
Budgie clicked on his radio. *Whrrr.* "Budgie to Control,
Budgie to Control. Lionel's out on a job and won't be
back for hours. Can we help? Over!"

"Control to Budgie. You and Pippa are much too light and small. We need Lionel's help. There's a storm brewing."

Budgie looked at Pippa. "Too small?" he said. "Who says we're too small? Too small for what?"

So Budgie listened to his radio to find out what had happened. Rose Wright, on her way home from school in Stanton, was stopped by some men in a car and bundled inside. Now the kidnappers wanted a huge ransom from her parents. Just as he was noting the description of the getaway car, Budgie's radio went dead. The sky grew very dark. The two friends had the same thought at once.

"Come on. Let's go."

Budgie felt the first drops of rain and heard the thunder. As he watched the lightning approach, he couldn't help feeling frightened.

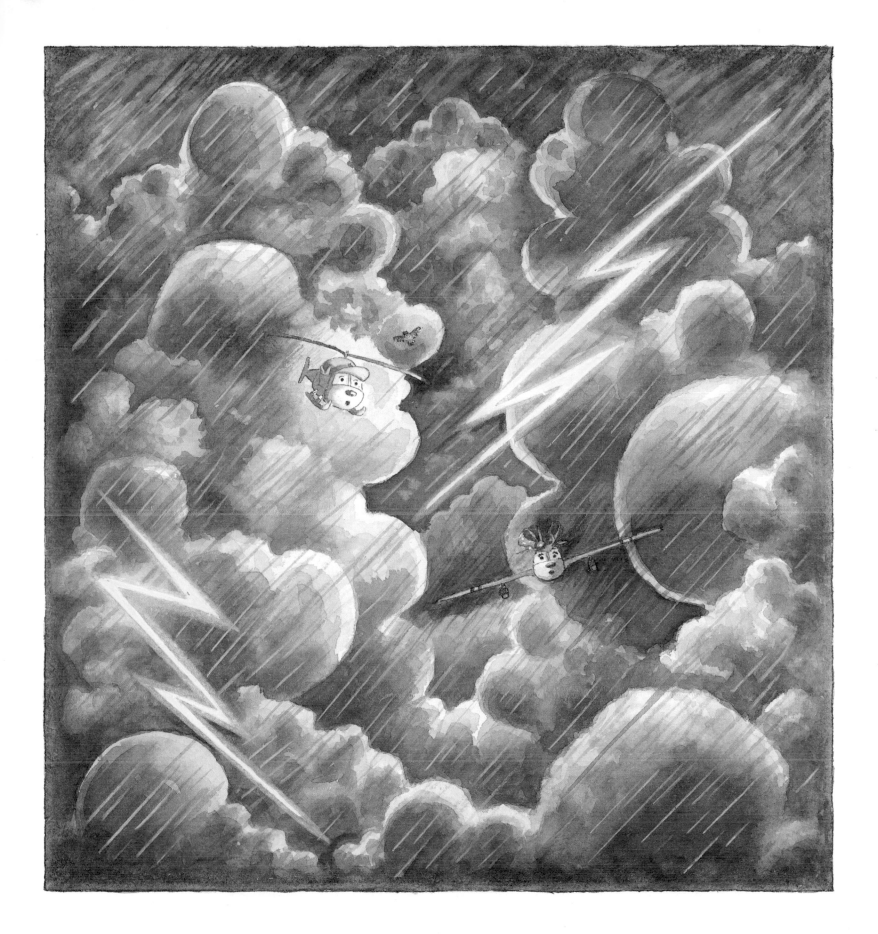

Buffeted and blown, Budgie and Pippa arrived at Stanton. They
spotted the school as the rain died away. They didn't know which
road the car had taken, so they flew in ever widening circles,
keeping fairly low. Then Pippa spied a big, black car in the distance.
"Quick," she said. "Let's follow them."

They followed the car for some time. Eventually it turned along a
country lane and headed towards an old barn. When the car stopped,
Budgie and Pippa flew straight past, pretending that nothing
was wrong.
"You keep watch, and I'll go for help," said Pippa. Silently she sped off.

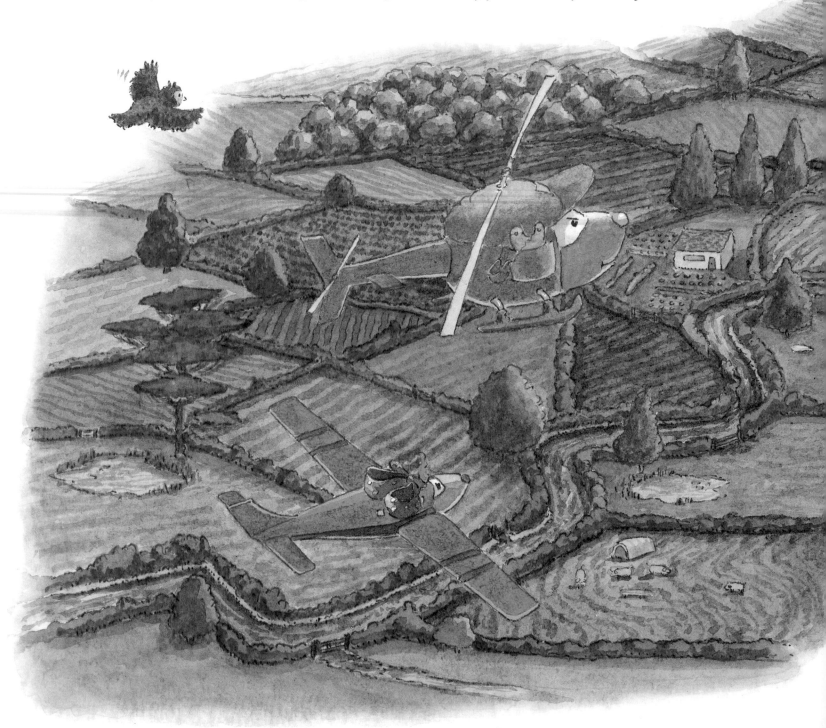

All alone, Budgie flew towards the barn. He turned off his engine and landed noiselessly. "Only a light and small helicopter could land between these trees," he thought proudly. As he watched and waited for help to arrive, it began to get dark.

Bang! Crash! There was a loud noise from the barn. Budgie looked up and heard a shout. "Get her."

"Over here, Rose!" Budgie shouted. "Look out, behind you. Quick, jump up!"
As quick as a wink, Rose was on board and Budgie went into action.

But just as Budgie lifted off the ground the man grabbed one of his skids and hung on.

"This is my chance," thought Budgie. "I'll keep him dangling until
the police arrive and arrest him. He can't escape."

Minutes later Budgie heard a screech of brakes. The police had
arrived and he heard a familiar clatter. It was Lionel barking orders.
The second kidnapper made a run for it.

"You won't get far," shouted Budgie.
  Then he carefully positioned himself over the roof of the barn.
"Here we go," he said as he shook his skids.

"Aaargh!" Crash! Bang! Splat!

Budgie landed gently and Rose jumped out. Her parents were waiting, happy and relieved that she was safe, and Rose ran towards them. Lionel looked on, smiling.

"Brave little Budgie saved me," cried Rose.

Budgie smiled. "What an exciting day it's been, after all," he sighed as he started for home.

Back at the hangar, Budgie received a hero's welcome.
"Good work, Budgie," said Lionel.
"I couldn't have done it without Pippa," said Budgie. "We make a good team."

"You'd better come with me," said Pippa mysteriously. "Now you're
a hero, you'll have to be cleaned up."
"Oh no," moaned Budgie. "It's nice being made a fuss of...

...but I hate taking a bath!"